# THE MIGHTY MACY

# KWAME ALEXANDER

# THE MIGHTY MACY

Illustrated by **KITT THOMAS**

**LITTLE, BROWN AND COMPANY**

New York Boston

This book is a work of fiction. Names, characters, places, and incidents are the product of the author's imagination or are used fictitiously. Any resemblance to actual events, locales, or persons, living or dead, is coincidental.

Copyright © 2026 by KA Productions, LLC | Illustrations copyright © 2026 by Kitt Thomas | Swirl pattern © 3d_kot/Shutterstock.com

Cover art copyright © 2026 by Kitt Thomas. Cover design by Karina Granda. | Cover copyright © 2026 by Hachette Book Group, Inc. | Interior design by Carla Weise.

Hachette Book Group supports the right to free expression and the value of copyright. The purpose of copyright is to encourage writers and artists to produce the creative works that enrich our culture.

The scanning, uploading, and distribution of this book without permission is a theft of the author's intellectual property. If you would like permission to use material from the book (other than for review purposes), please contact permissions@hbgusa.com. Thank you for your support of the author's rights.

Little, Brown and Company
Hachette Book Group
1290 Avenue of the Americas, New York, NY 10104
LBYR.com

First Edition: February 2026

Little, Brown and Company is a division of Hachette Book Group, Inc.
The Little, Brown name and logo are registered trademarks of Hachette Book Group, Inc.

The publisher is not responsible for websites (or their content) that are not owned by the publisher.

Little, Brown and Company books may be purchased in bulk for business, educational, or promotional use. For information, please contact your local bookseller or the Hachette Book Group Special Markets Department at special.markets@hbgusa.com.

Library of Congress Cataloging-in-Publication Data
Names: Alexander, Kwame, author. | Title: The mighty Macy / Kwame Alexander. Description: First edition. | New York : Little, Brown and Company, 2024. | Summary: "A young Black girl finds her voice and learns the power of advocating for herself and her community." —Provided by publisher. | Identifiers: LCCN 2023013032 | ISBN 9780316442169 (hardcover) | ISBN 9780316442381 (ebook) | Subjects: CYAC: Novels in verse. | Family life—Fiction. | Schools—Fiction. | Self-confidence—Fiction. | African Americans—Fiction. | LCGFT: Novels in verse. | Classification: LCC PZ7.5.A44 Mi 2024 | DDC [Fic]—dc23 | LC record available at https://lccn.loc.gov/2023013032

ISBNs: 978-0-316-44216-9 (hardcover), 978-0-316-44238-1 (ebook)

Printed in Indiana, USA

LSC-C

Printing 1, 2025

♪ ♫ ♩
**For Soleil and Indira**

# PIANO
(meaning "soft")

# Happy New Year

My birthday falls
on the first
of January
so my parents always gift
me something
that they want me
to do for the rest
of the year.

Today, I got
Book One of The Mighty Zora series
a journal with a lock and key
and a white dress
with red ribbons.

I guess they want me
to read more
write more
and go to school
dressed like Mary Poppins.

# *The Mighty Zora*

is about a twelve-year-old girl
who finds out she is the daughter
of a God and Goddess
which makes her a, yep, Goddess-
in-training, and her first class
is granting three wishes
and she's about to grant her first one
when Mom screams for me
to come downstairs
and I know what that means
and I *wish* I didn't have to practice violin
right now
because this book is
    unputdownable.

#  I wish

I was playing
with my bestie, Blue,
jumping rope
or skating
or laughing
or coloring with sidewalk chalk
or counting
clouds as they go by.

But instead
I'm playing violin
watching
through the window
while Blue
makes art
alone
and my
little brother JoJo
stands on
our front stoop

wearing the
red-and-blue
Super Rhyme cape
he made
as usual
practicing
for his weekly
rap battle
with Daddy.
> *Fifty-four TIMES*
> *I beat you with RHYMES*
> *You slip in my SPILLS*
> *You can't stop my SKILLS*

and his bestie—
Loud Jimmy—
hollers
about doing
something else.

Something else
sounds good
to me.

# A minuet

is a fancy dance
in triple time
> *squeak*

and my teacher always says
it's elegant
and dainty
> *creak*

and it's also a song
in my Suzuki violin
music book
> *screech*

and I'm playing
"Minuet 3"
in five days
at a recital
> *eeeek*

and it's my first solo
and I always mess it up
and have to start over
because I'm nervous

*shriek*

and I can't
read my new book
because Mom
told me
to practice

*scream*

and I need
this argument
with my violin
to end.

*squeak*

# My parents think

the word *homework* means
they have to give me
WORK
to do at
HOME
  (during THE HOLIDAYS)
when I could be
having fun
on a playdate
at the park
or in my comfy closet
finishing
the last five chapters
of *The Mighty Zora*
which is exactly what I was doing
beneath a clothes tent
when Daddy came in

saying it was time
to find my voice
and gave me an, UGH,
HOMEwork assignment.

# HOMEwork Assignment: Write an *I Am From* Poem

I am from orange high-top sneakers
and soccer cleats.
I am from Afros
and cornrows
(hair twisted tight
like spools of soft cotton).

I am from jeans
and cowboy boots
ice cream and lemonade.
I'm from summer bike rides
and no more car seats.

I am from Monopoly on Saturday nights
to violin every day.

From Daddy's favorite song
"Lift Every Voice and Sing"
to the lullabies
my momma sings at night
and the wake-up music she plays
in the morning.

I am from my grandmother's first name (Macy)
and my granddad's last name (Johnson).

I'm from so many books in my house
that our garage became a library.

Now can I get back to my book? Please?

#  No

Yes

Yes, I stayed up

Yes, I stayed up till 11:34 p.m.

Yes, I stayed up till 11:34 p.m. last night

Yes, I stayed up till 11:34 p.m. last night finishing the book

Yes, I stayed up till 11:34 p.m. last night finishing the book and I can't wait

Yes, I stayed up till 11:34 p.m. last night finishing the book and I can't wait to get Book Two

Yes, I stayed up till 11:34 p.m. last night finishing the book and I can't wait to get Book Two at the school library

But, Mom, can I please sleep
for ten more minutes?

# Good Morning, Macy

After Mom opens the curtains
and kisses me on the cheek,
she walks out and leaves my door open
so I can hear the sound of music
(Mom listens to Beyoncé
when she does her workout)
so I can smell
her blueberry pancakes
climbing the stairs
to my room.

I slowly roll out of bed
and walk into Daddy's room.
It's poetry time, I say.

He moans and mumbles
groans and grumbles
turns over
sees me climbing in
next to him
smiling and waiting
for a morning poem
because
my daddy is a poet.

# If you were an apple

*I'd peel you*
*I'd bake me a pie*
*and then meal you*

he says, both eyes still closed.

Meal me? That's funny, Daddy,
but what if I were something else
like maybe
a purple mountain?

*If you were a mountain*
*I'd climb you*
*Way up to the clouds*
*and I'd find you*

Daddy tries to tickle my feet.
I jump off the bed, grab a pillow
and it's wrestling time.
JoJo runs in, jumps on Daddy's head

and it's wild laughter time
and now we're all wide awake
then Mom yells
from downstairs:
**MACY**
    and
        **JOJO**

*Go brush your teeth*
    *Go wash your face*
        *Go put your clothes on*
            *Go*     *Go*     *Go*
like we're race car drivers
    and school
        is the finish line.

# Why I Need an Exterminator

I can't brush my teeth
wash my face
use the bathroom

(and I really have to
 GOOOOOOOOOOOO!!!)

because there's a pest
that we've had
for six years
and when he goes
into the bathroom
to take a shower
he doesn't come out
for an HOUR
and

DADDDDD, WILL YOU TELL JOJO
TO HURRY UPPPP.

# Tuesday

Before Daddy walks us
to school
like he does every day
    (when he's not traveling)
Mom says she loves us
and I say I love you too
then she says
*I love you three*
and Daddy stops us
'cause sometimes we all like
to love each other
to thirteen.

So she kisses me
    (and the pest)
on each cheek
and gives me
a super hug
that makes me feel

like she's the sky
and I'm a cloud
floating freely
in her arms.

# Along the walking path

to school
we pick up
Blue and

Loud Jimmy.

When we get to the crosswalk
before Daddy can start up
a lonnngggg conversation
with the crossing guard, Mr. Baker,
I stop him.

This is good right here, I whisper.
Third graders don't need parents
to walk them
across the street.

And even though
I do this every day
he still looks sadder

than Jimmy
in time-out.

So, I hug him
and run off to catch up
with Blue
'cause we're going to the library
to check out the next
Mighty Zora
before class starts.

# Cliffhanger

I wonder
what wish
Zora will grant next
because of course
Book One ended
right before the final wish.

Blue says if she could have any wish granted
she would fly to the moon
or give her grandmother a garden
that grew diamonds.

I would
wish I were
a little louder
but not as loud as Jimmy
a bit braver
but not always speaking like Daddy

sort of superhero-ish
but not wearing a cape like JoJo.

Maybe I'd be
Mighty
like Zora.

# A World of Words

Our school library
is a house
of hope
an imagination park
an opportunity store
a treasure chest
and right now
Blue and I
don't have the key
to get inside
this world of wonder
because when we arrive
there's a sign on the door
that says…

# CLOSED

*The school budget,* says
Ms. Marie Rose, our teacher,
*which is like*
*a big piggy bank*
*for all the schools*
*in our city,*
*has less money*
*in it*
*than it did*
*last year*
*and so each*
*school has to*
*cut back*
*on a few things.*
*Like the library?* Blue asks.
And Ms. Cooper, the librarian? I ask.

*Yes*, Ms. Marie Rose answers, *our library will only be open on Mondays and Fridays.*

# WHAT??!! I scream.

# Impatience

I may have to go
into my own piggy bank
and buy a copy
of the next book
because there's no way
I can wait until Friday
to find out Zora's third wish.

No way at all.

# Conversation with Blue

I'm so mad.
*Yeah, me too, Macy, but what are we going to do about it?*

Let's have a protest.
*How do we do that?*

My daddy took me to a rally last year. People were marching and chanting.
*Chanting what?*

"We're fired up, we can't take no more."
*Oh yeah! I saw that on TV. We just need some signs and a song.*

Then maybe we could boycott school.
*But we like school.*

We do.
*A lot.*

...
...

I'm gonna talk to my parents about it.
*Your daddy probably has a poem about this.*

Good idea. I'll ask him when I get home.
*They can't get away with this.*

They won't.
*Hey, Macy?*

Yeah?
*Are you gonna eat your fries?*

# Rituals

On Tuesdays after lunch
Mom does story time
in my class
and then we walk home.
If I don't
have Suzuki violin
or soccer practice
we jump in the car
and go straight
to the bread shop
for Apple Scrapple Muffins
then to the public library
where she volunteers
for an hour
every day
and I can lose myself
in a book
which hopefully will be
The Mighty Zora: Book Two.

But today
when Mom arrives
she's not alone.
Daddy's with her.

And he's wearing his blue suit and
shiny black shoes
which I don't like
because he only wears that suit
when he's getting on an airplane
which means that
today after school
instead of the bread shop
and the library
we're going
to the airport
and tomorrow
I won't have
Apple Scrapple
a new book
or Daddy.

# Surprise

The principal lets JoJo's class
join us for the read-aloud
since our parents are here.

*Hey, Mr. Macy's dad, won't you
    do a poem for us?* hollers Loud Jimmy.
*Yeah, about the color blue,* says Blue.

Our class is a circus.
Jimmy's jumping up and down.
Everyone's got ants in their pants

till Ms. Marie Rose tells us all
to sit snug
on the rug.

I plop down in the chair next to my daddy.
Read my favorite, I whisper.
*Not today, Sunshine,* he says. *Let's listen to
    Mommy's story.*

# PUHLLLEEEAAASSSEEE.

Do the fast one
that twists and turns
and rolls off your tongue

like a river of words.
*Okay, but only*
  *if you introduce me.*

No way! I think, shaking my head.
Blue gives me a thumbs-up, mouths
*You got this, Mace!*

Ladies, I whisper,
and other peoples, I whisper a little louder,
please—

*LOUDER*, Loud Jimmy screams
from the back of the room.
Welcome our favorite author to the stage, I say.

*Mo Willems is here?* Jimmy hollers again
which makes everyone laugh
except me and Daddy and Ms. Marie Rose

who dares him to make one more peep
or she'll send him back to his classroom.
Then Daddy jumps up

with a pretend microphone
like he's onstage
and we're the audience.

# My Favorite Poem

EBONY...
dark black and lovely **PROUD** BLACK

NIGHT black
outta **SIGGGHHHHHHT** black

soOOOOOOOOO black  **PURPLE** BLACK

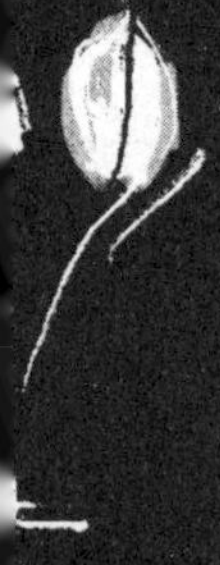

blue black black blue black black black blue black black
blue black black **black**

**brown**

smoked BLACK
*mellow yellow*
black BROWN

Chocolate *Brown* **Black**

**FRREEEEEEEEEEE** black

...IMAGES

#  Upset

I *love* that poem
and the class is in an **uproar**
but all I can think about
is how unfair it is
that Daddy's leaving
and that it's unlikely
he will make it to my recital
which of course makes me very

    u
       p
         s
           e
             t.

# MEZZO PIANO

(meaning "moderately soft")

# On the way to the airport

Daddy and Mom talk about getting new tires on the car…and how tasty our neighbor Gus's green tomatoes are…and how good Daddy's new book is gonna be…I want to ask them is this the book he wrote about me and my friends, but it's like they've forgotten I'm even back here…and JoJo is asleep and trying to use me as a pillow…and so I just clutch Daddy's navy-blue duffel…hum a song…and stare out the window…till somebody remembers they have a daughter…*I had fun reading to your class today…*I hum a little louder…*Don't be rude, Macy. Your father's talking to you…*Thank you for coming, I mumble, my head buried in my knees…*We're almost at the airport, can Daddy* *get a little smile...It's just that you need to promise you won't miss my violin recital on Friday evening...Nope, I'll be there. My plane arrives at 4:30, and your recital is at 5:30, so I'll be there. If I have to helicopter from the airport to the theater, you better believe I wouldn't miss it for anything...*Then he makes a funny face, and tries to get me to smile, and I almost do till I remember what else I'm angry about... But, Daddy, the library is closed and I can't get the next Mighty Zora and Ms. Cooper is probably sad and I want to save the library and I need an idea to get money and I don't have any ideas or enough money to save the library... and I need your help...and I thought we were gonna play basketball...and Loud Jimmy called me snooty again...and I don't know the title of your new book...and I like it when you listen to me practice violin...and how come we all can't fly away with you like we did that time to Maine...and how come grown-ups always get their way and children never do...And then Daddy takes off his seat belt...turns around...

and starts climbing in the back seat...and Mom says to him, *What are you doing?*...and Daddy flips like he's on the monkey bars...and now his bottom is hitting Mom on the side of her head... and he says, *Excuse my butt, darling*...and his head scrapes the floor...and now he's stuck... and JoJo wakes up and starts laughing...and I'm trying really hard not to laugh...and Mom says we're both nuts...and finally Daddy makes it to the back seat...and he hugs me...which makes me want to smile as big as the moon, but it's too late...We're at the airport...and then he whispers...*I'll miss you, Sunshine.*

#  I think

I'm coming down
with a cold.
I've got the sniffles
SNIFF SNIFF
so maybe I should stay home
from school tomorrow,
I tell Mom
COUGH COUGH
but she just keeps driving
and JoJo shakes his head.

*Mace, funny how you always get sick*
*after Daddy leaves. No one believes that. Geesh!*

I am telling the truth, JoJo, and now
my throat feels
a little scratchy.
SCRATCH SCRATCH, I add

and then Mom says
if I'm really feeling bad
she understands
but then we'll have to miss
pizza night
where we go to Mamma Leone's
the best pizza place on earth
and suddenly I don't feel
so sick
anymore…

# We get home and

Blue and Jimmy
are sitting on our stoop
waiting for us.

*I got a time-out
in class, for* **outbursts**,
yells Jimmy.

*What if Ms. Cooper
moves away
and we never
see her
or the inside
of the library
ever again?* asks Blue.

*I'm so hungry I could eat a whole chicken alone,
all the meat, and the bone!* says JoJo, high-fiving
Jimmy.

I can't believe
they closed
the library instead
of the
cafeteria, I say.
Books are healthier
than that nasty
food they serve.

*Ms. Marie Rose is mean,*
Jimmy whines.
*We are losing our librarian.
I'm hungry, too.*

This day was disastrous, I say.
We have to do something.
*YEAH!*

# Mamma Leone's

We walk into
the dimly lit and crowded pizzeria.

Sitting in a booth
by herself
holding a slice
of half-eaten pepperoni
in one hand
and her head in the other
is our librarian
trying to hide
her sadness.

# Snippets: Listening to a Conversation between Mom and Ms. Cooper

*Hello, Ms. Cooper,* says Mom. *I'm so sorry.*
*...kids need books.*

*They do...*
*...who will read...*

*Budgets shouldn't...*
*...so wrong*

*I know...*
*...*

*Ms. Cooper, how can we help?*
*...bored meeting Thursday.*

*...change their minds...speak up...*
*Oh, hi there, Macy. Read any good books lately?*

The Mighty Zora, but I can't get Book Two
because…It just seems so stup—
*Macy, watch your mouth.*

*It's okay, Macy's right. Sometimes adults make bad decisions. And closing the library was one of them.*
I just don't understand why, though.

*The school board needs to save money, so the solution is to cut some services.*
And children not getting to read is their solution?

*I don't think it is, Macy. But the school board has made a decision.*
It's just unfair. I'm sorry, Ms. Cooper.

…
*C'mon, Macy, let's give Ms. Cooper some peace. We should grab our pizzas and get back to the car before your brother does any damage.*

Bye, Ms. Cooper. See you on—
*Friday.*

Yeah…on Friday.

# After we finish eating

I practice
straight bow strokes
and tapping my toes
to get the tempo right
and forcing
my fingers to find their spots
and squinting
to see where the slurs are
and wondering...

What exactly is a **bored** meeting?

# Whenever Daddy goes

on one of his work trips
he writes poems
and hides them
in special places
for me to seek.

# Found Poem Taped to My Bathroom Mirror

*what's most important: you jojo mom us and then everything else*

# Mom says

*Honey, I love you,* then she
tucks me in
and spins a soft
bedtime song
that sends me
drifting halfway
into tomorrow.

# Wednesday

I backflip ten times
swim across a river
and just when I'm about to
jump over a school bus
I'm playing a violin concert
for The Mighty Zora
and Daddy
when the sun blazes
through my window
my eyes
and my dream.

Now all I want
to do is
get up
and jump
on Daddy's head
but he's gone,
so I pull the covers up
and dig my head

into the pillow
before Mom
starts with her
    Go
        Go
            Go

That's when I hear
something crackly
feel something crinkly
under my pillow.
A sheet of paper,
a secret from Daddy,
a morning poem.

# Found Poem under My Pillow

*Like Bessie Coleman*
*one day you're gonna fly, Sunshine,*
*like dawn wind*
*blazing through white clouds*
*soaring*
*into sunrise*
*like a little blackbird hopping*
*on a star*
*way up high*
*yeah, one day*
*you're gonna fly,*
*Sunshine.*

# In the middle of me practicing

JoJo yells:
*Mom, I'm sorry to HOLLER*
*But can I have a DOLLAR*
*To buy a snack at SCHOOL*
*Please, Mom, don't be CRUEL.*

*This is not a carnival, JoJo. Use your inside*
*voice*, Mom says.
*But I am INSIDE, and I'm ready to—*
he answers, but before
he can finish his rhyme, Mom gives him
the SEAL-YOUR-LIPS-AND-LISTEN
LOOK.

*Sunshine, good job with the minuet.*
*Sounds lovely.*
*Now, when you get to school, please*
*buy your brother a fruit snack, and*

*make sure it's unsweetened*, she says,
kissing me on the forehead.

C'mon, LANGSTON, I snap, putting my
violin in the case. Let's go to school.
*And, after school we can take a dip in the pool,
foo—*

But before he can finish, Mom gives him
the SAY-IT-AND-FIND-OUT-WHAT-
HAPPENS-NEXT LOOK.

A flyer on the wall
at school says

TEACHERS:

COME to the Board Meeting on Thursday. INSIST that the School Board RESTORE our students' bright future. REINSTATE THE SUGAR HILL LIBRARY BUDGET!

*Sincerely, The PTA*

# Class Chat

After morning announcements
Ms. Marie Rose says,
*Since Library Day is canceled...*

As soon as she says LIBRARY
twenty-five hands shoot up
and wave around in the air.
Ms. Marie Rose sighs
and calls on us
one at a time.

*Library Day is my favorite.*
*Are you going to read us a story? (Yes.)*
*I miss Ms. Cooper.*
*Me too.*
*They shouldn't cancel Library Day.*
*Why did they close the library? (Money is low.)*
*Will it ever be open every day again? (I hope so.)*

*Will we still have Read Across America Day?*
   *(I don't know.)*
*The library can have my lunch money.*

It went on
and on
until it was
almost recess
and finally my turn
to ask a question.
What is a Board Meeting?
*It's a meeting where our leaders share information
   and talk about policies and plans.*
Sounds boring.

*And make decisions.*
Oh.

Before I get
the courage
to lift my voice

to say I saw the flyer
and ask if kids can go
to Board Meetings
the recess bell
rings.

# Found Poem in My Lunch Bag

*If you were a bun*
*I'd grilled cheese you*

*I'd hug you for lunch*
*and then freeze you*

*I'd thaw you at night,*
*then cuddle real tight*
*and thank you for letting me*
*squeeze you.*

*Love, Daddy*

(So silly!)

# Hatching a Plan

After me and Blue
finish reading and giggling,
she asks, *So, where
did your daddy go
this time?*

To a museum in Montgomery, Alabama,
to read a poem about civil rights.
*Our library closing is uncivil rights.*

We're at lunch
talking
with our mouths
full.

The PTA
made a flyer.
I saw it
on the wall.

They want
teachers
to go to
the Board Meeting.
I think
we should go, too,
I say.

*Good idea!*
yells Jimmy.

*Everyone should GO
and sit in the front ROW,*
adds JoJo.

*I can make
posters tonight,* offers Blue,
*to tell kids
to come.*

And
we can get an adult,
one of our parents maybe,
to speak up
about our rights.

Or

*Why not you?* Blue asks. *You could speak up.*

# Not Me

All three of them grin
and nod and clap for me and
my very big mouth.

# Too Much

A minuet
A plan
 full of posting posters
 and getting to school early
 to spread the word
 at the drop-off curb TOMORROW.
A Board Meeting TOMORROW
and now
talking
in front
of a bunch
of strangers.

TOMORROW?

Nope.
Not.
Never.

It's just too much.

# Suzuki Violin Lesson

I have four fingers
that won't play in three-quarter time.
Maybe I should quit.

This song is too fast
and it has too many notes.
Maybe I should quit.

It's embarrassing.
Practice does not make perfect.
Maybe I should quit.

Teacher taps her foot,
hums the harmony, and says,
*Don't give up, Macy.*

Maybe she reads minds.

# Mom, Please?

*First,*
*finish your salad*
*scrape your plate*
*put the dishes*
*in the dishwasher*
*sweep the floor*
*wash your hands*
*clean your face*
*give me a hug*
*practice for ten minutes.*

*Then, yes*
*you can go outside*
*and play*
*for half an hour.*

# Friends

JoJo finds me
and Blue and Jimmy
lying in the front yard
staring
at the sinking sun.
*Y'all wanna play, while it's still today?*
    he raps, and plops down next to me.
No thanks, I'm too stressed out,
    I answer, thinking about how much I miss
    Daddy, and the library.
*What y'all see up there anyway, birds,*
*   airplanes, heaven?*
    hollers Jimmy, tickling me with one hand
    eating popcorn with the other.
*She's trying to find her smile,*
    Blue answers, putting my hand in hers.
*Knock, knock,* says Blue.
WHO'S THERE? screams Jimmy.
*Cows say,* says Blue.

*Cows say who?* asks JoJo.
*No, silly, cows say Moooooo!*
and before you know it,
we're all knock-knocking
and laughing
and holding hands
and looking up
at the silvery moon
about to spoil
all our fun
'cause it's almost time
to go in.

# How NOT to Write a Poem

Sit in your closet
with the headset light
your grandma gave you
for Christmas.

Hold your pencil
and your favorite purple journal
in your hands
while your brain refuses to cooperate
and you have no ideas
and no clue
what to write
until you start humming a song that you know
'cause it's Daddy's favorite:

*Sing a song full of the faith that the dark past has
    taught us,*
*sing a song full of the hope that the present has
    brought us*

And then you feel a raindrop, a few words
begin to sprinkle onto the page,
and you wish you didn't hear Mom
coming up the steps
to tell you *Lights out!* Because
if you just had a little more time
you know that a monsoon
of metaphors and messages
would come bursting out of nowhere
and everywhere
and a rainbow of words
would be splattered across this page.

But it's bedtime.

# Sweet Dreams

I'm lucky
I have
a best friend
who cheers
me up
and a mom
who piles
pillows
around my head
and pulls
a quilt
up to my chin
and sings
"You Are My Sunshine"
softly
    until
        I
            d r i f t
                    into
                          tomorrow.

# CRESCENDO
(meaning "gradually louder")

# I wake up...

and remember
today is Thursday
and I need
to meet Blue
before school
to put up posters
and spread the word
about our uncivil rights plans
and I *need to write a poem*
to lift my voice, I guess,
because
today is
the B-O-A-R-D Meeting
but I don't
really want to…

# I go...go...go

through my morning
routine of rushing.
Then after breakfast
as soon as I lick
the last drop
of organic maple syrup
from my fork
Mom jets
outta nowhere
and makes me
practice
"Minuet 3"
on my violin
for fifteen miserable minutes.

# Daddy never drives

us to school
but JoJo's Hour of Shower
and my "Minuet 3"
made us late,
so Mom
tells us
to hop in the car
because she has to teach
her exercise class in thirty minutes
and she seems
*stressed*
and I think
maybe
she misses
Daddy
as much as
I do.

# Chaos

In front of the school
there is a line
of cars
as long as
Daddy's trip,
and Loud Jimmy
is running
up and down
the sidewalk
SHOUTING
*Come to the Board Meeting tonight!*
*Save the library!*
Blue is waiting,
holding the posters
she made at home last night
and waving one hand
at me.
*Hurry up,*
she mouths
while JoJo

rolls down the window
and screams at Jimmy,
telling him to say
*Let's put up a FIGHT*
*at the meeting TONIGHT!*
Then Mom says,
*Thank goodness—a spot,*
and swerves
to the curb
and I practically
tumble over.
Jimmy opens the door
and I stumble
into
my day.

# Ladies and everybody else

says Blue,
*I present to you
Macy Johnson!*
When I don't
speak
JoJo and Jimmy
giggle.
Blue repeats herself
and
I
have
to
admit,
There is no poem

yet.

# Drowning

I need a floaty
or a life jacket or a
quiet library.

# Wondering

One time
I couldn't choose a book,
so Ms. Cooper
recommended some
and she didn't stop
until I found one.

*Baby-Sitters Club*
I've read that

*Junie B. Jones*
Same

*Ryan Hart*
Finished last week

*A book of poems by Langston Hughes*
Cool! JoJo's real name is Langston

I miss
Ms. Cooper
and her book
recommendations.
I wonder what
she would recommend
for someone who has to write
their own poem.
I wonder what
she would recommend
for me today.

# Ms. Marie Rose Is Making Us Write Letters in *Cursive*

Dear Daddy,

How are you? What are you doing?
I miss you and I'm glad you're coming
    back for my recital
but I think that might be too late because
I really need you to be here today
because I started writing a poem
but I haven't finished
and I still can't play "Minuet 3"
and I've never given a speech
and my speech is supposed to be a poem
is supposed to be ready for the Board
    Meeting tonight
and there will be a ton of people staring at
    me and listening to my poem
but I don't know what they'll be listening
    to because there is no poem

and how can I help Ms. Cooper get her job
   back
and keep the library open if I can't write?
And even if I had a speech I think
I'd be too nervous to say it.

Do you ever get stage fright?
I bet you don't

but I have stage fright times two because
of the meeting and the minuet
and I said I'd do both things
and I don't want to do either one
and if you were here I know you would
   help me
but you're not.
I guess I could ask Mom
but she doesn't do public speaking unless
she is teaching Zumba public speaking
or maybe public Y E L L I N G?
I'll be glad when you get back
and you can make up a morning poem
about if I was something that I'm not
like a poem giver
or a minuet player.

I love you, Daddy.

Love,

Macy

# I finish

my letter early
so I take out my birthday
journal and I find…

# A Found Poem

*A place for your words,
a place for your thoughts, where you
can become...yourself.*

# False Starts

Ladies and children and fathers and others,
I would like to ask…
People of the Board, can you please…
Dear Decision Makers, I INSIST that you
   MUST…
Good evening, I love the library and…
Hola! Yo estoy a student at Sugar Hill…
Hello, my name is Macy and I need Book
   Two…
Hey! Why did you take money from my school
   library?!?!

Dearly Beloved, we are gathered here today to
   shake our heads at this poem speech…

# Serious Magic

I thought
I needed
Daddy but
I might need
Mary Poppins
because it's gonna take
some serious
magic
to make this thing
I'm supposed to be writing
save our
*supercalifragilisticexpialidocious* library.

# Help?

On our walk home
I take
Mom's hand
and whisper,
I need help.

*What's wrong?*
I don't have a poem.

*You have a few hours before the Board Meeting.*
But I need to practice "Minuet 3."

*You can do it, Sunshine.*
Mom, can YOU give a speech instead?

*No, baby, your voice is more important. Lift it,
    remember?*
Too heavy.

...

Maybe you can ask my violin teacher if I can
>  play "Twinkle, Twinkle" at the recital this
>  weekend instead?

*Macy, you made a commitment.*
But, Mom, it's too much.

*Challenge makes you strong. Confidence makes*
>  *you stronger.*
This conversation is making me weak.

*Challenge is GOOD*
*I think you SHOULD*
*Stick to your WORD*
*So you can be HEARD!*
says JoJo.

Mom, can you
please
tell JoJo to SHU—

But before I can continue, Mom gives me a
DON'T-YOU-DARE-SAY-THAT-TO-
YOUR-BROTHER LOOK.

*JoJo, give your sister some space to think.*

In the quiet, I think
and hope.

And worry

A LOT.

# If Daddy were here

he would
spin me a poem
and tickle my funny bone
and fold me into a hug
and sneak me a chocolate kiss
and lift me to the clouds
and I'd grow wings
and

               Y
           L
    F

# FORTE

(meaning "loud")

# An orchestra

is a group
of musicians—string,
woodwind,
brass,
and percussion—who come together
to play
a symphony.

Hmmm.
What if I did
a symphony of

WORDS!

# Mom is playing
## *Sinfonia Americana*

by the spectacular composer
Damien Geter
when the idea
appears
in my brain
and it's like
someone
turned on
the light
and it's bright,
a gleaming star
and it's loud even,
as a rolling sea
and now
I see
what was

already there
high as the glistening sky
and I know what I'm gonna say
and this poem is gonna SHINE!

# Standing Room Only

One time
we went to church
for Easter
and every spot
on every pew
was taken
and I had to sit
on Daddy's lap.

I guess
we did a good job
spreading the word
because church on Easter
was empty
compared to
this Board Meeting.

OH MY!

# JoJo & Blue Introduce Macy

*Here is my SISTER*
  *Glad you didn't MISS HER*

*Mace always reads BOOKS*
  *on pillows in NOOKS*

*She wrote a big SPEECH*
  *and is ready to PREACH*

*Mace Johnson, please STAND*
  *Y'all GIVE MY BESTIE A HAND!*

# OH MY!

heart thumping
hands sweaty
blood pumping
unsteady…

Not…quite…ready…

B R E A T H E

and

say…

# Sinfonia Libraria
# (My Symphony)

I love the library
and, as you will hear,
so do all my friends
who shared these words
with our class:

*The library*
*is almost*
*as good as*
*Grandma's house.*

*Now where
am I supposed
to go
when I feel sad?*

*I don't like
books,
but I like the library
because Ms. Cooper
never
yells at us.*

*When I read
in the library
I forget
I'm at school.*

*Are the books lonely?*

*One time
I fell
asleep in the library
and Ms. Cooper*

*wasn't even
mad.
She said
I must have
needed it.*

*I love Ms. Cooper.
The library has
a million books
and Ms. Cooper
knows
where they all are.*

*How
are we
supposed
to read
the books?*

*One time
I found
a book and
the boy in it*

*looked
just like me.*

*I love books.*

*Ms. Cooper
changes
the decorations
every month.
The library
feels like
Christmas.*

*I love
the Book Fair.
Are they taking
that away,
too?*

*One time
Ms. Cooper
let me*

*stay after school
when
Mom was late.*

*Ms. Cooper is nice.
She reads us stories.
Library Day is my favorite.*

*Will we still have Read Across America Day?
What would Dr. Seuss say about your budget?*

*I love to read.*

*I love the library.
I love Ms. Cooper.
I love books.
I love to read.*

*Closing the library
was
a bad
idea.*

*Why did they
take money
from
the library?*

*The library can have my lunch money.*

*Will they
ever
change
their
minds?*

*Maybe tonight
they will.*

We all love our library.

# Standing Ovation

Clap
     Clap
CLAP, CLAP, CLAP
*ClapClapClapClapClapClapClap.*

People on
their feet

cheers
whoops
hollers
and one loud
*THAT'S MY SUNSHINE!*
from Mom.

# I did it

without Daddy
without Mom
without The Mighty Zora
to grant me three wishes
    or two
    or one
with nothing
but
the words of many
and the voice of me:
## The **Mighty** Macy.

# No Stopping for Me

One more
mountain
to climb and
Mount Minuet
is mighty steep.

If my
fingers ache
and my
eyes dry out
and my
arm trembles
and my notes
shatter the windows
I will keep
climbing,
keep practicing.

Case open.
Violin out.
Get ready
to rosin my bow
then find another
poem from Daddy.

# Found Poem in My Rosin Compartment

*The Mighty Zora*
*ain't got nothin' on you—you*
*are always the Queen.*

#  Yes!

No
No, I did not
No, I did not go to bed
No, I did not go to bed at bedtime
No, I did not go to bed at bedtime because I needed to practice
No, I did not go to bed at bedtime because I needed to practice "Minuet 3"
No, I did not go to bed at bedtime because I needed to practice "Minuet 3" so I don't sound bad
No, I did not go to bed at bedtime because I needed to practice "Minuet 3" so I don't sound bad, and now I sound AMAZING!

And, can you believe
I'm not even tired?

# Before Mom

can even
open her mouth
to say
>Go
>>Go
>>>Go

or JoJo
gets a chance
to slide
into the
bathroom
I'm up
dressed
and eating oatmeal
while Bill Withers
sings
about a bright
sunshiny day.

And I know that *sunshine* is ME.

# It Worked!

Ms. Cooper's back
with hellos
and smiles
and hugs
and news that the library
IS BACK OPEN
EVERY EVERY EVERY
 DAAAAAAAAAAY
and thank-yous
and a box
of new books
including
the
whole
entire
Mighty
Zora
series!

# Attention

My whole day
is high fives
and *good-job*s
and *way-to-raise-your-voice*s
and *thank-you*s
and *you-were-so-brave-last-night*s
and one
*You are a hero!*

# Is School Over YET?

Ticktock
    Ticktock
I watch the clock
through the glass
but time won't pass

So much to say
and play
and Daddy's coming home
TODAY!
I
    can
           not
                wait
tonight will be
GREAT!

# Snippets: Listening to a Conversation between Mom and Daddy on the Phone

*Hi...*
*...What?*
*...Why?*
*...Is there another flight?*
*...(sigh)...*
*...Okay, well...*
*...try...*
*Love you, too...*

*...bye.*

# Delayed

It's not Daddy's fault
that he broke a huge promise
he shouldn't have made.

# Mary Poppins

White dress with red
ribbons, lace, and Daddy's love
gets full when I twirl.
My mind and heart, both spinning,
especially when JoJo says, *Pretty!*

# Peeking

out from the wings
stage left
red curtains
hide me
but they can't hide
the empty seat
between
JoJo and
Mom.

# Spotlight

When the orchestra finishes
playing Beethoven's
"Minuet in G"
I walk up
to the front
in my new dress
and take a bow.
*And now
a solo by Macy,* says
my teacher.
*She will play
"Minuet 3."*
The piano starts
which is my cue
to play
and I say
to myself
I GOT THIS.
And I do

and Mom is
smiling
and so
am I,
a little.

Then I hear a cough
from the very back
of the room
and look up to see
my
# DADDY
grinning so big
I can count
his teeth
and I add
a little
extra
vibrato
just because
I can.

# Applause

I tuck
my violin
under
my arm
raise my bow
in the air
and take
another bow.

Cologne fills my
nose up
as Daddy
scoops me up,
lifts me
like a ballerina,
then gives me
a bear hug
before we
go home.

# Spoonful of Sugar

The next morning
I climb
into bed
with Daddy
for a poem.

He smiles
and spreads his arms
for a
pre-poem hug.

*If you were a poem*
*I'd write you*
*with rhythm and rhyme*
*and recite you.*

Before I can say a word
the smell
of something sweet
climbs the stairs.

At the
same time
we say,
*Chocolate chip pancakes?!*

And we
     Go
          Go
              **Go**
like race car drivers
because Mom
almost never
gives us
sugar for breakfast.

Life is
sweet!

# Author's Note

The idea for this story wouldn't have happened if Steph hadn't had the bright idea to enroll our daughter, Samayah, in Suzuki violin lessons. And I wouldn't have been compelled to write this story if I hadn't sorrowfully missed some of those lessons and recitals because I was traveling. And there's no way this book would've been published if not for the thoughtful encouragement, brainstorming, and writerly guidance from my dear friend Nikki Shannon Smith.

# KWAME ALEXANDER

is an Emmy Award–winning producer and the #1 *New York Times* bestselling author of over forty books, including the Newbery Medal–winning novel *The Crossover*; the Caldecott Medal– and Newbery Honor–winning picture book *The Undefeated*; *The Door of No Return*; and *J vs. K*, which he cowrote with Jerry Craft. He invites you to visit him at kwamealexander.com and @kwamealexander.

**KITT THOMAS**, also known as Katelan, is the #1 *New York Times* bestselling illustrator of *Stacey's Extraordinary Words* by Stacey Abrams and *Cape* by Kevin Johnson. A first-generation St. Lucian American, Kitt is a two-time NAACP Image Award winner and a graduate of Ringling College of Art and Design. Kitt's mission is to celebrate Black culture with their drawings and to encourage inclusion in all forms of art. They live in Cincinnati, Ohio. Kitt invites you to find them on social media @kitt.thomas.art.